House mouse

Barrie Watts

A & C Black · London

Here is a mouse.

Have you ever seen a house mouse in your home or garden?
They often live in houses, especially during the winter when
it is cold and wet.

This drawing shows four different types of mice.

harvest mouse

house mouse

wood mouse

pet mouse

What differences can you see between them?

This book will tell you how a house mouse is born
and how it grows up.

*A CIP catalogue record for this book
is available from the British Library.*

ISBN 0–7136–3380–8

Published by A & C Black (Publishers) Limited
35 Bedford Row, London WC1R 4JH

© 1991 Barrie Watts

Acknowledgements
The artwork is by Helen Senior.
The publishers would like to thank Michael Chinery for his help and advice.

Filmset by August Filmsetting, Haydock, St Helens
Printed in Belgium by Proost International Book Production

The mouse comes out at night.

House mice are very shy and do not like people.

They usually sleep in the daytime and come out
to look for food at night when no one is about.
These are some of their favourite foods:

cheese

sunflower seeds

wheat grains

bread

Mice have strong sharp teeth and can easily nibble
their way into food packets. When they are hungry
they will eat almost anything, even soap.

Can you see what the mouse in the photograph is eating?

The male and female mate.

Look at the drawing. The male and the female mouse are mating. Soon baby mice will start to grow inside the female.

The female mouse in the photograph has mated with a male and is pregnant. She is getting very fat and needs plenty of food and water.

Twenty days after mating with the male mouse, the female is ready to give birth.

The babies are born.

When the female mouse is ready to give birth she makes a cosy nest. She uses any warm material she can find and tears it up into small pieces.

Look at the photograph. These mice have just been born and are each about the size of a small grape. They are blind and deaf and have no fur.

A female usually has a litter of about eight babies. How many baby mice can you see in the picture?

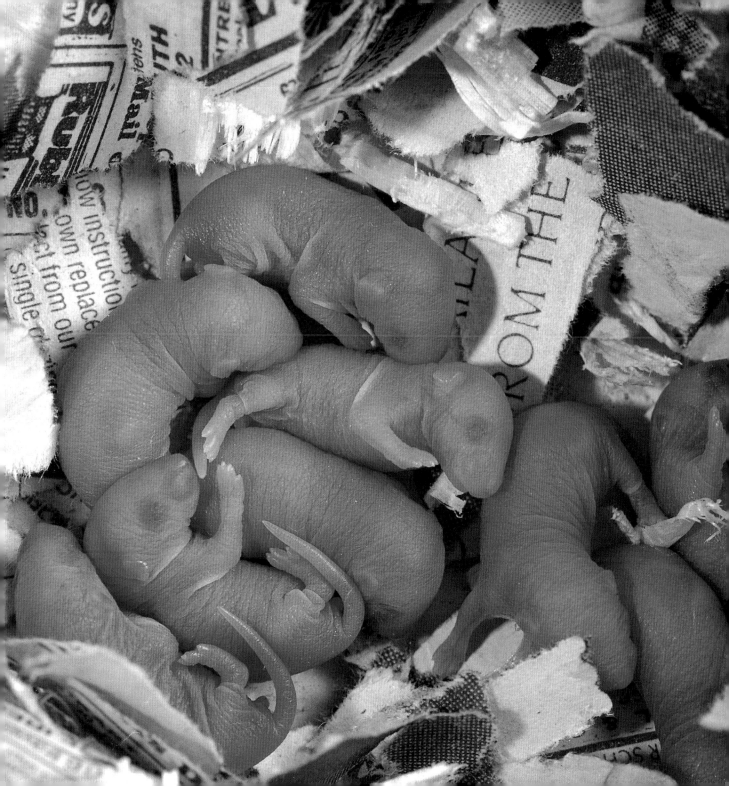

The mother feeds the babies.

The mice in the photograph are four days old.
Their pink skin is slowly disappearing under
a layer of grey fur.

Look at the drawing.

These mice are a week old. They are feeding on
their mother's rich milk. They suck the milk from
teats on her stomach.

The babies are two weeks old.

At two weeks old, the baby mice have all their fur and can open their eyes. They keep warm in the nest by moving around or snuggling up close to one another.

The baby mouse in the small photograph is still only about the length of a matchbox. Its tail is almost as long as its body.

The young mice are three weeks old.

At three weeks old, the mice can see properly for the first time. They begin to explore their surroundings and play with their brothers and sisters.

They talk to each other by making high-pitched squeaks which we cannot hear.

The young mouse comes out of the nest.

Although the mother continues to find food for her babies, she is no longer giving them milk, and soon they start to leave the nest to look for their own food.

The mouse in the drawing has found a sunflower seed. It holds the seed with its front paws and nibbles with its sharp teeth.

The young mouse looks after itself.

After six weeks, the young mouse is big enough to move a long way away from the nest to look for food.

It begins to explore all over the house and garden, but especially in the kitchen. Here it climbs on to shelves and into cupboards to look for food.

The young mouse also spends time cleaning itself. The mouse in the big photograph is using its front paws to clean its face.

The mouse can climb well.

As the mouse gets older it is able to climb, jump and even swim. It is also very good at balancing.

Look at the mouse in the small photograph.

Its long scaly tail is sticking out straight behind it to help it balance on the rope.

The young mouse is fully grown.

After two months, the young mouse is almost as big as its mother. It is old enough to live on its own and will have moved a long way away from its mother and the nest where it was born.

If a female mouse meets a male mouse they will mate and the female will become pregnant.

What do you think will happen then?

Do you remember how a house mouse is born and grows up?
See if you can tell the story in your own words.
You can use these pictures to help you.

Index

This index will help you to find some of the important words in the book.

There might be mice living in your home or garden.
Look out for mouse droppings and nibbled food packets.